不朽的美

大风起兮云飞扬

许渊冲经典英译诗词

（周朝——六朝）

第一辑：汉英对照

Songs of the Immortals

AN ANTHOLOGY OF CLASSICAL CHINESE POETRY (I)

Translated by Xu Yuan Zhong

许渊冲 译

新世界出版社
NEW WORLD PRESS

First Edition 2019

Translated by Xu Yuan Zhong
Designed by He Yuting

ISBN 978-7-5104-6279-5

Published by
NEW WORLD PRESS
24 Baiwanzhuang Street, Beijing 100037, China

Distributed by
NEW WORLD PRESS
24 Baiwanzhuang Street, Beijing 100037, China
Tel: 86-10-68995968
Fax: 86-10-68998705
Website: www.nwp.com.cn
E-mail: nwpcd@sina.com

Printed in the People's Republic of China

INTRODUCTION

I

"Chinese literature," according to John Turner in his *Golden Treasury of Chinese Poetry*, "is the high artistic peak of the most literary, the most artistic, the longest-established civilization that exists." The earliest anthology of Chinese literature is *The Book of Poetry*, consisting of 305 poems and compiled in the sixth century BC. It is divided into three main sections: 160 songs, 105 odes, and 40 hymns. The songs are folk songs collected by royal musicians from fifteen feudal states that clustered along the Yellow River; the odes are ceremonial or festive songs composed by official diviners and historians and used before going to war and hunting; the hymns are songs of praise and advice to the ruler, written by officials and used as part of ancestral sacrifices and feasts during the Western Zhou period from the eleventh to the seventh centuries BC.

The poems center on daily activities. We see people farming and hunting (*Hunting*), gathering food and courting (*A Fair Maiden*), performing sacrifices and going off to war (*Comradeship*). Poems about love and marriage form the bulk of the folk songs, presenting the sadness and joy of lovers' partings and reunions, as well as the relative freedom of love in those days for ordinary people (*The Quiet Maiden*).

Many of these poems are light-hearted in tone, but others complain of unhappy love affairs or marriages (*A Faithless Man*), misrule or the hardships of soldiering (*Homecoming after War*). The happier songs tend to express feelings directly while the unhappy singer often turns to metaphors. For example, the poet vents his indignation against injustice on earth by enumerating the stars in heaven which do not live up to their fine names:

In southern sky appears a Winnowing Fan,
Alas! It can't be used to sift the grain;
In northern sky a Dipper, which man,
Alas! Would use to ladle wine in vain.

The poem's depth of feeling and unusual artistic technique are remarkable for the Western Zhou period.

Structurally, each line of these poems is made up of four characters (*Homecoming after War*), though lines of other lengths occur at times. The lines are arranged in stanzas, usually of four lines each (*The Rooster Is Crowing*). Rhyme is used at the end of the even-numbered lines. Alliteration, assonance, and inner rhyme are also used. Many songs employ, repetitions (*My Man's Away*) and refrains, others start a stanza by evoking an image quite apart from the central theme (*The Fruits from Mume Tree Fall*), a device called "evocation" or "association." Conciseness is also a feature of the earliest Chinese poetry.

As *The Book of Poetry* was numbered among the Five Confucian Classics, it has had considerable influence because of its use as a basic text in traditional Chinese education.

II

If *The Book of Poetry* is the earliest anthology of realistic songs composed by the northern people, *The Verse of Chu* (also translated as *Elegies of the South*) may be said to be the earliest collection of romantic poems written by a southern intellectual, Qu Yuan (340-278 BC). During Qu Yuan's life, northern realism met southern romanticism. Qu Yuan's blending of the two made him the greatest lyrical poet in the period of the Warring States (475-221 BC). His best-known work is his autobiographic long poem *Sorrow after Departure*, which depicts his grief at being estranged from the undiscerning King of Chu. He refers to the king as "Fair One" and "Godly One," and compares his own longing for a discerning king to the quest for an ideal mate. Thus he established in classical Chinese poetry the tradition of using beauty to symbolize the sovereign and fragrant plants to represent loyal ministers and subjects. He writes:

I did not grieve to see sweet blossoms die away,
Grieved rather that amid weeds they did decay.

His love for the ideal is so deep that he says:

Long, long the way, I know not which to go.
I'd seek my heart's desire both high and low.

He could not bear the grim reality and drowned himself in the Miluo River on the fifth day of the fifth lunar month, which has become the Dragon Boat Festival in his memory.

Other poems attributed to Qu Yuan include *Nine Hymns and*

Nine Elegies. The former are songs dedicated to gods or goddesses and written in a form suggestive of drama, in which a male or female shaman donned elaborate costume and make-up, singing and dancing, and invited the god or goddess to an amorous encounter. As sacrifices to the gods were occasions for courtship, thc mention of love in these hymns is natural, whether love between man and woman, god and goddess or god and mortal. In *To the God of Cloud* the songstress professes love for the god; in *To the Lord of River Xiang* the god courts the goddess; in *To the Lady of River Xiang*, a lovesick goddess is portrayed in dramatic form. In Chinese poetry love between gods comes after that between man and woman, as opposed to the Greek epic in which the romantic comes before the realistic. There is only one hymn which makes no mention of love, which is the poem praising fallen warriors. In that hymn there is no celebration of heroic deeds and feats of arms usually associated with the epic poetry of the West. *In Ode to the Orange*, one of the *Nine Elegies*, we find the image of an ideal man.

Qu Yuan uses in *Nine Hymns* and *Nine Elegies* a line of four, five or six characters, broken in midline by the insertion of a breathing particle "xi" and concluded (usually) with end rhyme. This form is known as Southern Song style.

III

By the end of the period of the Warring States, the King of the Qin State in the northwest had conquered all the other states and founded in 221 BC the Qin Dynasty with the king as its first emperor. During his reign scholars were buried alive and classics burned so that no literature was left. About a thousand years later the Tang poet Zhang Jie (837-?) wrote a satirical quatrain called *The Pit Where Emperor Qin Burned the Classics*:

Smoke of burnt classics gone up with the empire's fall,
Fortress and rivers could not guard the capital.
Before the pit turned cold, eastern rebellion spread;
The leaders of revolt were not scholars well-read.

The leaders of the revolt were General Xiang Yu of the State of Chu and Liu Bang who defeated Xiang in 202 BC and founded the Han Dynasty (206 BC-AD 220). But it was not the victor but the defeated hero and his beautiful Lady Yu who were glorified in poetry later. For example, Li Qingzhao (1084-1151) wrote the following quatrain:

Be man of men while you're alive;
Be soul of souls e'en though you're dead.
Think of Xiang Yu who'd not survive
His men, whose blood for him was shed.

Lady Yu's name became the title of a song sung from generation to generation. Is it not an irony of history?

During the Han's four hundred years of relative peace and stability, literature and learning flourished after Confucian doctrines had formed the official foundation of the state and the civil service examination system was established under the reign of Emperor Wu or Liu Che (156-87 BC). Lyrical works were composed in the Southern Song style that derived from the *Nine Hymns* of *The Verse of Chu*, and used a six or seven-character line broken in the middle by the breathing particle "xi." Emperor Liu Che wrote in this form too. But, at variance with the emperor, later poets sang the praise more of his disfavored general than of His Majesty. For instance, Lu Lun (c. 748-c. 800) described the feats of General Li Guang in his *Border Songs*:

In gloomy woods grass shivers at wind's howl;
The general takes it for a tiger's growl.
He shoots an arrow at a shape in view,
Only to find at dawn a rock pierced through.

Besides the works assigned to known authors, we have anonymous folk songs which take their name from a government office called the Music Bureau, set up around 120 BC by Emperor Wu to collect songs from various parts of the empire. These songs reflect the life and hardships of the common people. Some use lines of irregular length and others use predominately five-character lines, a form which reached its climax during the High Tang period.

IV

Chinese history has been marked by a recurring cycle of unification, division and reunification. The Han Dynasty founded by Liu Bang in 206 BC was overthrown in AD 220 and the unified empire split into the Three Kingdoms of Wei in the north, Shu in the west and Wu in the south. The Wei Dynasty was set up by Cao Cao (155-220), who was not only a warlord but also a poet who continued the tradition of *The Book of Poetry* and wrote in the old four-character verse form. His eldest son Cao Pi succeeded him on the throne, continued the tradition of *The Verse of Chu* and became one of the earliest poets to write in seven-character verse form. Cao Zhi (192-232), younger brother of Cao Pi, was well-known for his literary talent, particularly his five-character verse, which won his father's favor when Cao Zhi was only ten years old and provoked the jealousy of his elder brother, who ordered him, under penalty of death, to write a five-character verse while taking seven paces; it reads:

Pods burned to cook peas,
Peas weep in the pot:
"Grown from the same trees,
Why boil us so hot?

A nice example of the poet's wit under pressure, this poem along with the many others composed by Cao Pi, Cao Zhi and their father have established the place of the Three Caos, as they are known in the history of Chinese literature.

In 208 Cao Cao was defeated at Red Cliff by Sun Quan, king of the State of Wu, and Zhou Yu, commander-in-chief of the Wu navy, whom Su Shi (1037-1101) described as follows:

I fancy General Zhou Yu at the height
Of his success, with a plume fan in hand,
In a silk hood, so brave and bright,
Laughing and jesting with his bride fair,
While enemy ships were destroyed as planned
Like castles in the air.

The exploits of Liu Bei, king of Shu, and his Prime Minister Zhuge Liang were also glorified in later poetry, for example, by Du Fu (712-770) in *The Temple of the Famous Premier of Shu*:

The emperor thrice called on him for nation's sake;
The famous premier served heart and soul for long years.
Before victory was won he died, which would e'er make
All heroes after him wet their sleeves with hot tears.

For Chinese intellectuals, Zhou Yu has become the image of an ideal general who can win victory against heavy odds, and Zhuge Liang an ideal minister whose life is entirely devoted to the interest of the nation.

Besides works about kings and princes, ministers and generals, there were also popular ballads such as *A Pair of Peacocks Southeast Fly*, composed around 220. This is a long narrative poem telling how the feudal ethics of the patriarchal clan system destroyed the happiness of a young couple, who were unable to overcome it except in death.

V

The Three Kingdoms were reunified in 265 by the Jin (265-420), but the decay and collapse of the Han had in some degree discredited the Confucian doctrines and cleared the way for a revival of interest in the transcendental thought of Taoist philosophers. During the Wei and Jin Dynasties most scholars tried to escape reality and the best-known poet was Tao Qian (c. 365-427), who retired from official life to a pastoral life of farming and writing and became the archetype of the "hermit poet." Many of his poems described the quiet joys of country life, for instance:

Among the haunts of men I build my cot,
There's noise of wheels and hoofs, but I hear not.
How can it leave upon my mind no trace?
Secluded heart creates secluded place.
I pick fence-side chrysanthemums at will
And leisurely I see the southern hill.

But other poems spoke of famine, drought and similar hardships. The Taoist side of his nature told him he should be content with such a life of seclusion, but his dedication to Confucian ideals kept him longing for the less troubled times of the past when virtue prevailed and a scholar could in good conscience take an active part in state affairs. Unable to attain his ideal, he sought solace in wine and verse, writing in a plain and simple style in a five-character verse form.

In 420 the Jin Dynasty was replaced by the Song, and the empire was split into the Northern and Southern Dynasties (420-589). The Southern emperors worshipped Buddha and built hundreds of Buddhist temples so that Buddhism exercised a predominant influence during the Six Dynasties. This can be seen in the following quatrain:

Orioles sing amid red blooms and green trees;
By hills and rills wineshop streamers wave in the breeze.
Four hundred eighty splendid temples still remain
Of Southern Dynasties in the mist and the rain.

The poets of that period excelled at describing natural sceneries. For example, Xie Tiao (464-499), whom Li Bai (701-762) admired, wrote the following five-character lines:

I see from distance high and low
Winglike tiled roofs in sunset's glow.
The colored clouds spread like brocade,
The river calm as silver braid.

In 589 the Northern and Southern Dynasties were both overthrown by the Sui (589-618), and the well-known *Song of Mulan* appeared, a poem about the first Chinese war heroine, which symbolizes the reunification of the North and the South. But the Sui was a short-lived dynasty, whose second and last emperor was notorious for his life of luxury. The poetry of this period tended to be shallow and mannered, ornate in diction and much given to the use of rhetorical devices such as parallelism, allusion and elegant variation.

VI

The Tang Dynasty (618-907) was the golden age of Chinese poetry. It may be divided into four periods: Early Tang (618-712), High Tang (713-770), Middle Tang (771-835) and Late Tang (836-907). Early Tang poetry followed the ornate style of the Six Dynasties, but some poets began to break the tradition. For instance, Yu Shinan (558-638), whom the emperor highly appreciated, wrote the following five-character quatrain called *The Firefly*:

You shed a flickering light;
Your wings are weak in flight.
Afraid to be unknown,
At night you gleam alone.

Later, Wang Bo (c. 649-676) and three other poets tried to develop a style of their own and were criticized by their contemporaries. But Du Fu wrote the following seven-character quatrain in support of them:

Our four great poets have their own creative style;
You shallow critics may make your remarks unfair,
But you will perish with your criticism, while
Their fame will last as the river flows fore'er.

It was Chen Zi'ang (661-702) who succeeded in infusing new vitality into the tradition of the Six Dynasties by returning to the spirit of Han and Wei poetry. He was regarded as a precursor of the High Tang poets.

The High Tang period represented the peak of poetic excellence in the Tang Dynasty. It corresponds roughly to the reign of Emperor Xuan Zong (712-755), a ruler whose early years on the throne were marked by power and splendor and who, as a worshipper of Confucius, wrote the following five-character verse while offering sacrifices to him:

For what did you so busily strive, my Sage,
Expounding hard your doctrine in your age?

Even his favorite Lady Yang could write poems and the following is her seven-character quatrain *Dancing*:

Silk sleeves are swaying ceaselessly with fragrance spread;
In autumn mist are floating lotus lilies red.
Light clouds o'er mountains high ripple with breezes cool;

Young willow shoots caress water of garden pool.

During the reign of Xuan Zong, all civil service examination candidates were required to compose a regulated verse, so poetry became an indispensable accomplishment and a daily accompaniment to the lives of officials and scholars.

Among the High Tang poets, Wang Changling (698-756) was well-known for his seven-character quatrains, in which we can see the influence of the Six Dynasties palace poetry. The following quatrain on a disfavored court lady is typical:

She brings her broom at dawn to dust the golden halls
And strolls about with round fan within the palace walls.
Her rosy color envies wintry crow's black one,
Oft bathed in favorable light of royal sun.

Instead of describing the luxurious palace life in flowery poetic style, this quatrain reveals the poet's sympathy with a disfavored lady whose beauty could not even outshine the ugly crow, so it reads more like *Lament of the Autumn Fan* of the Han Dynasty than a palace poem of the Six Dynasties.

Wang Wei (701-761) was the most important pastoral poet of the High Tang period, best known for his five-character poems. He was a devout Buddhist, a fact that deeply influenced the way in which he viewed the world and his place in it. As a celebrator of the quiet joys of rural life, he followed a line of development earlier explored by Tao Qian, though he wrote with greater calm and detachment than

Tao. For example, his *The Dale of Singing Birds* reads as follows:

I hear osmanthus blooms fall unenjoyed;
When night comes, hills dissolve into the void.
The rising moon arouses birds to sing,
Their fitful twitters fill the dale with spring.

He did not assiduously seek out the picturesque elements in the natural landscape, but rather registered the scenes about him just as they appeared. No wonder it is said "in his poetry there is painting and in his painting there is poetry."

VII

Li Bai was the best-known poet in Chinese history, a representative of High Tang culture, the combination of Northern culture represented by Confucian philosophy and *The Book of Poetry* and Southern culture represented by Taoist philosophy and *The Verse of Chu*. His life may be summed up by the following quatrain *To Li Bai* written by Du Fu:

When autumn comes, you're drifting still like thistledown;
You try to find the way to heaven, but you fail.
In singing mad and drinking dead your days you drown.
For whom will fly the roc? For whom will leap the whale?

Li Bai could not fulfil his Confucian ideal to serve the country, spending his later years wandering lonely like a drifting cloud. Nor could he find spiritual freedom in Taoism which taught him to seek the way to heaven. He could but chant poetry and drink wine to drown his sorrows as described by Du Fu in *Eight Immortal Drinkers*:

Li Bai could turn sweet nectar into verses fine.
Drunk in the capital, he'd lie in shops of wine.
Even imperial summons proudly he'd decline,
Saying immortals could not leave the drink divine.

In Li Bai we have the tragedy of a lonely genius wandering the earth like an angel fallen from heaven. When would he realize his aspiration to fly to the sky like the fabulous roc mentioned by the Taoist philosopher Zhuang Zi?

Li Bai's poetry is marked by masculine grandeur (*Watching from Afar the Waterfall on Mount Lu*) and natural grace (*The Moon over Mount Brow*). His imagery may be sublime (the giant bird symbolizing his love of freedom) or graceful (the moon conveying his sympathy to his banished friend Wang Changling). His description of natural scenery is characterized by a swift and fierce imaginative sweep. For instance:

Oh, lightning flashes
And thunder rumbles;
With stunning crashes,
The mountain crumbles.

But he disappoints when describing human feelings and always compares them to natural phenomena. For example:

However deep the Lake of Peach Blossom may be,
It's not so deep, O Wang Lun! as your love for me.

He is little given to expressions of despair or bitterness. His poetry on the whole is calm, at times sunny in outlook. It appears to grow out of certain convictions that he held regarding life and art, out of a tireless search for spiritual freedom and communion with nature as in Poem (*Sitting Alone Facing Peak Jingting*), a lively imagination and a deep sensitivity to beauty (*A Reply to Someone in the Hills*).

Peach blossoms fallen on the running stream pass by;
This is an earthly paradise beneath the sky.

VIII

Du Fu was as great a realistic poet as Li Bai was a romantic. As Li was called "Poet Immortal," Du was remembered by posterity as the "Poet Sage" or "Poet Historian" because he had mirrored in his works the world he lived in and revealed himself with candor and passion. While Li cherished now Confucian then Taoist ideal, Du was imbued with a strong Confucian sense of duty that compelled him to continue serving the Tang Dynasty in the hope of assuaging the ills of the nation. His poetry describes the grief as famine and misrule were inflicting upon his countrymen on the one hand and reproaches those who were responsible for the misery on the other. For instance, he wrote on his way from the capital to Fengxian the following well-known couplet:

The mansions burst with wine and meat;
The poor die frozen in the street.

Li Bai also reproached men in power, but he only said:

How can I stoop and bow before the men in power
And so deny myself a happy hour?

These two examples clearly show Li as subjective and romantic and Du as objective and realistic.

The same is true of their descriptions of natural scenery. They both wrote about mountains, but we find in Li's *Mount Skyland* an imaginary mountain "surpassing the Five Peaks" in height, and in Du's *Mount Tai* (one of the Five Peaks) "one boundless green out-spread two states." They both described the Yangtze River, Li as "the endless river rolls beyond the azure sky," a view only the mind's eye can yield, while in Du "the endless river rolls its waves from hour to hour," in a description obvious to everyone. They both sailed through the Three Gorges; we find in Li only his own joy, while in Du not only the joy of his family but also that of all the people returning to their homes in the recaptured regions. They both wrote about clouds and birds, but in Li's *Peak Jingting* we seem to see the poet lonely as the cloud and free as the bird, while in Du's *Mount Tai* the poet is only an observer of the rising clouds and the fleeting birds. They both described rain, but Li did not like to see it coming "from dark, dark cloud," while Du felt happy to see it "mutely moisten all."

In expressing feelings, Li was more personal and Du more sympathetic. Both of them felt lonely, but Li was detached in his solitude while Du could not free himself from his attachment to the Tang Dynasty, and this is one of the essential differences between them.

Among other High Tang poets, Cen Shen (715-770) was well-known for his frontier verse ("The frozen red flag in the wind won't undulate"). His ballads with descriptions of the harsh climate and rough terrain of the frontier stand in marked contrast to the pastoral poems of Wang Wei.

IX

If the Early Tang and High Tang periods may be likened to the spring and summer of a year, then the Middle Tang can be compared to autumn, the season of harvest. The revolt of An Lushan in 755 had a disastrous effect on the economic and political life of the Tang Dynasty and it never recovered its former stability. In keeping with the changed nature of the times poetry took on an increasingly autumnal air. On the one hand, Wei Yingwu (737-789) followed the tradition of pastoral poetry (*On the West Stream at Chuzhou*) and on the other, Li Yi (748-827), that of the frontier poems (*On Hearing a Flute at Night atop the Victor's Wall*). But their poetry had not the tone of exuberance that had marked the earlier decades.

The most important poet of the Middle Tang period was Bai Juyi (772-846), who mingled Du Fu's realistic tradition with Li Bai's romanticism (*The Everlasting Regret*), but he also made innovations and wrote "New Music Bureau Ballads" in a style marked by deliberate simplicity (*The White-Haired Palace Maid*). He himself placed high value on his poems of social criticism such as *The Red Cockatoo*:

Annam has sent us from afar a red cockatoo;
Colored like peach-tree blossom, it speaks
as men do,
But it is shut up in a cage with bar on bar
Just as the learned or eloquent scholars are.

This seven-character quatrain, which reveals the relationship between the ruler and the ruled intellectuals, acts more upon the reason than the emotions and may be considered a forerunner of the didactic poetry of the Song Dynasty. Another seven-character quatrain which reveals the Buddhist influence on the poet reads as follows:

Studying the Buddhist doctrine of emptiness, I find
The way to still all common states of mind....

But the great Buddhist influence revolted another Confucian innovator Han Yu (768-824), who submitted to the emperor a memorial in which he reprimanded His Majesty for his devotion to Buddhism and was exiled eight thousand miles away (*Written for My Grandnephew at the Blue Pass*).

Bai Juyi was the most prolific of the Middle Tang poets. As Liu Yuxi (772-842), he composed "Bamboo-Branch Songs" and "Willow-Branch Songs," which are early forms of tuned poetry, that is, a poem or lyric written to a certain tune whose title refers simply to the metrical pattern and in most cases has nothing to do with the poem's content. The tuned lyric marked by lines of varying length came to prominence in the Middle Tang period. For example, Zhang Zhihe's (730-810) *Fisherman's Song* was so widespread that even the Japanese emperor (r. 804-832) wrote five lyrics to the same tune. Zhang's lyric is pastoral, Liu's *Ripples Sifting Sand* realistic and Bai's *Flower in the Haze* symbolic.

X

Li He (790-816) who followed the romantic tradition of Qu Yuan and Li Bai, and whose rich, allusion-laden poetry is obscure and even depressing, may be regarded as a precursor of Late Tang poets. If the major poets of the High Tang were Li Bai and Du Fu, then those of the Late Tang were another Li and Du, that is, Du Mu (803-852) and Li Shangyin (812-858).

Du Mu has shunned in his poetry "the ornate and the strange" on the one hand and "the commonplace and the vulgar" on the other. His seven-character quatrains are admired for their visual immediacy and delicacy of feelings. For instance, one of his farewell poems reads:

Deep, deep our love, too deep to show.
Deep, deep we drink; silent we grow.
The candle grieves to see us part;
It melts in tears with burnt-out heart.

Li Shangyin was perhaps the most influential of all the Late Tang poets. His seven-character regulated verse reads like Du Fu's and Han Yu's in syntax and structure, and like Li He's in diction and allusiveness. He is well-known for his ambiguous or obscure poems, often untitled, dealing with clandestine love. He was the first poet to write love poems in the modern sense and has left to posterity such unforgettable couplets as:

The silkworm till its death spins silk from lovesick heart;
The candle when, consumed has no more tears to shed.
The setting sun appears sublime,
But O! 'Tis near its dying time.

The second couplet may be said to be the epitome of Late Tang poetry.

Wen Tingyun (813-870) was the most important lyricist or composer of tuned lyrics of the Late Tang; he transformed them from mere songs of entertainment to verses of high literary quality. In his lyrics two main styles are predominate: a richly embellished depiction of the abandoned woman as opposed to the court lady in the palace poem, and a simple narration in the folk song manner as represented by *Dreaming of the South.*

Wei Zhuang (836-910) was another important lyricist of the period of transition. His tuned lyrics are straightforward, narrative and colloquial, directly expressing personal feelings and autobiographical details as opposed to Wen's indirect depiction of feminine feelings. What he adds to the tuned lyric reveals a reaction against the ornate style of Wen, who excels in writing poems with implicit meaning, while Wei is famed for explicit poetry.

In 881, Huang Chao (?-884) led an army of sixty thousand peasant rebels into the Tang capital and proclaimed himself emperor. He expressed his ambition in *The Chrysanthemum*, with whose "golden armor plates" came the end of the Tang Dynasty.

After the downfall of the Tang in 907, five short-lived dynasties were successively founded and overthrown from 907 to 960, and the unified empire was dismembered into ten independent sovereign states, of which the State of Shu in the west and that of the Southern Tang in the east were well-known for their literary achievements. When the regulated Tang verse could no longer adequately express man's more refined and delicate feelings, the tuned lyric of irregular line-length took its place and evolved into a major literary genre during the Five Dynasties. The literary aspect of the tuned lyric was derived from the five-character and seven-character lines of the regulated verse, the musical aspect from the popular songs and the tunes introduced from Central Asia, India and Myanmar. For example, *The Buddhist Dancers*, one of the most popular tunes, was said to be a song in praise of the hairdress of the Myanmar empress of the time. So the tuned lyric may be considered as a result of intercultural communication.

As mentioned above, the states of Shu and Southern Tang were two cultural centers during the Five Dynasties period. In the former the first anthology of tuned lyrics appeared in 940, most of which can be called boudoir poetry in that it described beautiful heart-broken women in elegant chambers keeping cold, lonely beds beside a dimming candle or a solitary screen, in the waning spring or the dead of night, their lovers having gone far, far away.

Li Yu (937-978), the last ruler of the Southern Tang (937-975), represents the highest achievement of the lyric poets during the Five Dynasties period. His unusual accomplishment was closely related to his personal experiences. In his early years, as monarch, he indulged in a luxurious life at court. After losing his kingdom to the Song emperor in 976 and becoming a political prisoner in the Song capital, he lived a life of suffering until his death. His tragedy may be summed up in his tuned lyric written to the tune of *Dance of the Cavalry*, in which the expanse of his lost kingdom symbolizes the limitless extent of the universe and the short history of his dynasty becomes a universal symbol of the time past. The dominant theme in his lyric is no longer confined to the experiences of the inner chamber, but extends to embrace the historical dimension of a kingdom and the vast expanse of an empire. His individual experiences seem to gain universal importance. When compared with Wen and Wei, Li's poetry is more universal. Wen's lyrics are descriptive and static, Wei's narrative and active, while Li's more personal and emotional verses seem to view his own suffering in light of the destiny of all mankind. If Wen's lyrics are written with colored ink and Wei's with bitter tears, then Li's are composed of his heart's blood.

XI

The tuned lyrics predominant in the Five Dynasties were short tunes divided into two stanzas and contained no more than 62 characters. The lyricists of the Northern Song (960-1127) included high officials and even prime ministers, who brought poetry into closer contact with the life of prosperous society in all its aspects-secular, intellectual and artistic. Premier Yan Shu (991-1055) and his son Yan Jidao (1030-1106) were both good at composing short tunes. Professor Chia-ying Yeh, who calls the son "poet of feeling" and the father "poet of intellect," says in *Song without Music*: "The one responds passively to life, registering experience as pure feeling; the other does not simply experience reality, and he contributes a ray of understanding to his experience. The response of the former suffers from its narrowness, where the latter has the advantage of breadth. Where the response is purely emotional, the poetry conveys emotion but lacks thought, making for superficiality, while the one who can illuminate his subject will include thought with his feelings, and the result is greater depth. Consider these lines by Yan Shu: "Deeply I sigh for faded flowers' fall in vain/Vaguely I seem to know the swallows come again." The observation of seasonal change is not just the occasion for an emotional response. The poet perceives a pattern, a contrast or a repetition, that gives a rational basis for the emotion.

Yan Shu may be regarded as the leader of early Northern Song poets, among whom figured Fan Zhongyan (989-1052), well-known for the quote that an ideal minister should be "first in worrying about the troubles of the world and last in enjoying its pleasures," and also known for his frontier lyrics. Ouyang Xiu (1007-1072), who sought spiritual sublimation in prose and emotional satisfaction in verse, was successful in enlarging the themes and the language of love poetry.

The short lyrics these poets wrote were as restricted in form as in content, for the restriction in form had its impact on content. It was Liu Yong (987-1053) who began to compose long lyrics or slow tunes, whose length ranges from 70 to 240 characters and which afford sufficient room for undulation and amplification. With the skilful use of this diversified form, he was able to transcend such conventional motifs as sorrows of love or remorse over separation and diverge from the domestic and the personal by giving voice to a deeper and more complex layer of meaning, to a wider horizon of the spiritual world, such as the sense of desolation and loftiness evoked by watching distant places in *Eight Beats of Ganzhou Song.* Thus in his hand the spirit and the outlook of the tuned lyric underwent a radical change, the rise of the long tunes becoming a major event in the evolution of the lyric.

The most important poet and lyricist of the Song Dynasty was

Su Shi (Su Dongpo, 1037-1101). If the development of the tuned lyric in form may be attributed to Liu Yong, then its growth in content must be credited to Su Shi, who created the lyric in the mode of Tang poetry and in so doing broadened its scope and elevated its status to the extent that "there is no idea which cannot be expressed and there is no subject which cannot be treated" in his lyrics. His style is exuberant and spontaneous, characterized by his virile, unrestrained nature. His poetic diction ranges from colloquialism to classical expressions. His philosophy represents a combination of Confucianism and Taoism: "to serve the crown and to attain great renown" (*Spring in the Garden of Qin*) is his Confucian ideal and "to retire as times require" (*ibid*), and to be detached from gain and loss, his Taoist ideal. His philosophy can be seen in the following long lyric written to the tune of *Congratulations to the Bridegroom*:

Young swallows fly along the painted eaves
Which none perceives.
The shade of plane-trees keeps away
The hot noonday
And brings an evening fresh and cool
For the bathing lady beautiful.
She flirts a round fan of silk made,
Both fan and hand as white as jade.
Tired by and by,
She falls asleep with lonely sigh.
Who's knocking at the curtained door
That she can dream sweet dreams no more?

It is the gentle breeze who
Is again swaying green bamboo.
The pomegranate opens half her lips
Which look like wrinkled crimson strips;
When all the fickle flowers fade,
Alone she'll be the Beauty's maid.
How charming in her blooming branch, behold!
A fragrant heart seems wrapped a thousand fold.
But she's afraid to be surprised by western breeze
Which withers all the green leaves on the trees.
When you come to drink to the flower fair,
To see her withered too you cannot bear.
Then tears and flowers
Would fall in showers.

The bathing beauty is no longer the abandoned lady of palace poems, but an image of the purified soul of the disfavored poet still dreaming of his ideal unfulfilled, the pomegranate a symbol of the purified lady envied by all the fickle flowers. Here we see three images combined into one, that of a disappointed but not disillusioned intellectual.

Su Shi was considered to be the leader of the "heroic" school of lyrics, but he was also an innovator in writing lyrics of "delicate restraint," and Qin Guan (1049-1100), one of his followers, was regarded as representative of the "delicate" school. He was well-known for the following couplet:

If love between both sides can last for aye,
Why need they stay together night and day?

On the other hand, Zhou Bangyan (1057-1121), one of Liu Yong's followers, inherited the form from the master while at the same time surpassing his achievements. "While Su Shi remained an observer in creating a metaphorical relation between external objects and universal human feelings, Zhou developed a situation of poetic empathy in which the lyric self maintains a symbolic correspondence with external objects" (Kang-i Sun's *Evolution of Chinese Tz'u Poetry*). It is interesting to note that Zhou was once the rival of Emperor Hui Zong (Zhao Ji, 1082-1135) for the love of a singing girl Li Shishi (*Wandering of a Youth*). The emperor was himself a lyricist and wrote *Apricot Seen in the North* to the tune of *Hillside Pavilion* when he was a captive sent to the north by the Jurchen invaders. The descendant of the Song emperor who had captured Li Yu and put him to death was in turn captured and put to death by the Jurchen aggressors. Is it not true to say that justice has a long arm?

XII

In 1125, when the Jurchen invaders marched south, the Song was forced to move its capital from Kaifeng to Hangzhou, south of the Yangtze River, which marked the beginning of the Southern Song Dynasty (1127-1279). Many patriots spoke out against the humiliation and called for military action to remedy it, thus Southern Song poetry possessed a patriotic fervor, of which General Yue Fei's (1103-1141) *The River All Red* is typical.

Li Qingzhao (1084-1151), who lived in the intervening period between the Northern and Southern Song, was the most remarkable lyric poetess of the Song Dynasty. Her lyrics recollect nostalgically her happy life in Kaifeng and reveal her distress in Hangzhou. "Her attempt to establish life in poetry was for her a stay against time, a surety to blot out oblivion. She tried to recapture the past, to preserve the present...." (*Sunflower Splendor*).

Lu You (1125-1210) was the best-known patriotic poet of the Southern Song. Even on his deathbed, he wrote the following quatrain exhorting his sons not to fail to report to his spirit at family sacrifices the news of the eventual recovery of the lost territory:

After my death I know for me all hopes are vain,
But still I'm grieved to see our country not unite.
When royal armies recover the Central Plain,
Do not forget to tell your sire in sacred rite!

Xin Qiji (1140-1207) was regarded as the most important lyric poet of the Southern Song Dynasty. He was a successor to Su Shi, continuing his thematic emphasis while at the same time putting a tighter rein on prosody than his master. It was not until his appearance that the tuned lyric flourished and reached its apex. His reputation as the best lyric poet of the "powerful and free" school rests on his heroic sentiments expressed in such lyrics as *The Partridge Sky and*

Dance of the Cavalry.

On the other hand, among the lyric poets of the school of "delicate restraint," the best-known were Jiang Kui (1155-1221) and Wu Wenying (1200-1260). Successors to Zhou Bangyan, they had certain common features, such as their painstaking choice of words and phrases, and the great attention they paid to the music and the description of subtle feelings. But the content of their poems tended to be ambiguous, empty, and full of ornate classical allusions. As the tuned lyric became more and more concerned with technical details of embellishment, it gradually lost its vitality.

Towards the end of the Southern Song, the best-known poet of the "heroic" school was Wen Tianxiang (1236-1282), prime minister who led the royalist army to fight the Tartar invaders in 1275. Defeated and captured, he wrote the following verse on his way to Yanjing (present-day Beijing):

But I'll come back with blood oozing in cuckoo's cry.

He was executed in 1282 and with his death came the end of the Southern Song Dynasty.

XIII

During the one century of Mongol rule in the Yuan Dynasty (1271-1368), new musical melodies and new poetic genres emerged: song-poems, or non-dramatic songs, and dramatic songs. The new forms admit freely the use of everyday colloquial speech, the idiom and slang of the common people and extra words in addition to what was required by the melody. Writers of non-dramatic songs were skilled in their descriptions of sceneries and situations, persons and objects (though sometimes trivial and humorous) and thoughts and sentiments. But as a whole, the song-poem is basically lyrical in nature. On the other hand, dramatic songs are not only lyrical but also narrative. The most important writer of dramatic songs was Wang Shifu whose *Romance of the Western Chamber* contains a narrative part in prose and a lyrical part in verse. So the Yuan Dynasty may be considered one of transitional periods from predominance of poetry to that of prose. During the Ming Dynasty (1368-1644), narrative prose predominated over lyrical poetry, and it was not until the appearance of *A Dream of Red Mansions* in the Qing Dynasty (1644-1911) that the lyrical became as important as, if not more important than the narrative, but that question goes beyond the scope of the present book.

ZHOU DYNASTY

(1046-256 BC)

周朝

（前 1046—前 256）

THE BOOK OF POETRY (770-476 BC)

A Fair Maiden

By riverside are cooing
A pair of turtledoves;
A good young man is wooing
A maiden fair he loves.

Water flows left and right
Of cresses here and there;
The youth yearns day and night
For the good maiden fair.

His yearning grows so strong
He cannot fall asleep;
He tosses all night long,
So deep in love, so deep!

Now gather left and right
The cresses sweet and tender;
O lute, play music bright
For the bride fair and slender!

Feast friends at left and right
On cresses cooked so tender;
O bells and drums, delight
The bride so fair and slender!

诗经

（前 770 – 前 476）

关雎

关关雎鸠，在河之洲。
窈窕淑女，君子好逑。

参差荇菜，左右流之。
窈窕淑女，寤寐求之。

求之不得，寤寐思服。
悠哉悠哉，辗转反侧。

参差荇菜，左右采之。
窈窕淑女，琴瑟友之。

参差荇菜，左右芼之。
窈窕淑女，钟鼓乐之。

The Fruits from Mume Tree Fall

The fruits from mume tree fall,
One-third of them away.
If you love me at all,
Woo me a lucky day!

The fruits from mume tree fall,
Two-thirds of them away.
If you love me at all,
Woo me this very day!

The fruits from mume tree fall,
Now all of them away.
If you love me at all,
You need not woo but say!

摽有梅

摽有梅，其实七兮。
求我庶士，迨其吉兮！

摽有梅，其实三兮。
求我庶士，迨其今兮！

摽有梅，顷筐塈之。
求我庶士，迨其谓之！

My Quiet Maiden

My quiet maiden is fair and tall;
She waits for me at the corner wall.
Evasive, she can be found nowhere;
Scratching my head, I seek here and there.

Beautiful is my quiet lass;
She gives me a blade of crimson grass.
The crimson grass spreads a rosy light;
I love the grass so fair and bright.

My maiden comes back from the mead;
She gives me a beautiful rare reed.
It's beautiful not because it's rare;
But it's the gift of my maiden fair.

静女

静女其姝，
俟我于城隅。
爱而不见，
搔首踟蹰。

静女其娈，
贻我彤管。
彤管有炜，
说怿女美。

自牧归荑，
洵美且异。
匪女之为美，
美人之贻。

The Faithless Man

A man seemed free from guile,
In trade he wore a smile.
He'd barter cloth for thread;
No, to me he'd be wed.
We went across the ford;
I'd not give him my word.
I said by hillside green,
"You have no go-between.
Try to find one, I pray.
In autumn be the day!"

I climbed the wall to wait
To see him pass the gate.
I did not see him pass;
My tears streamed down, alas!
I saw him passing by,
I'd laugh with joy and cry.
Both reed and tortoise shell
Foretold all would be well.
"Come with your cart," I said.
"To you I will be wed."

氓

氓之蚩蚩，抱布贸丝。
匪来贸丝，来即我谋。
送子涉淇，至于顿丘。
匪我愆期，子无良媒。
将子无怒，秋以为期。

乘彼垝垣，以望复关。
不见复关，泣涕涟涟。
既见复关，载笑载言。
尔卜尔筮，体无咎言。
以尔车来，以我贿迁。

How fresh were mulberries
With their fruits on the trees!
Beware, O turtledove,
Eat not the fruits you love,
For they'll intoxicate.
Do not repent too late!
Man may do what he will,
He can atone it still.
The wrong a woman's done
No man will e'er condone.

The mulberries appear
With yellow leaves and sear.
E'er since he married me,
I've shared his poverty.
Desert'd, from him I part,
The flood has wet my cart.
I have done nothing wrong;
He changes all along.
He's fickle to excess,
Capricious, pitiless.

桑之未落，其叶沃若。
于嗟鸠兮，无食桑葚。
于嗟女兮，无与士耽。
士之耽兮，犹可说也。
女之耽兮，不可说也。

桑之落矣，其黄而陨。
自我徂尔，三岁食贫。
淇水汤汤，渐车帷裳。
女也不爽，士贰其行。
士也罔极，二三其德。

Three years I was his wife
And led a toilsome life.
Each day I early rose,
And late I sought repose.
He thought it not enough
And began to become rough.
My brothers did not know,
Their jeers at me would go.
Mutely I ruminate
And then deplore my fate.

I'd live with him in vain;
I had cause to complain.
I love the ford of yore
And the wide river shore.
When we were girl and boy,
We'd talk and laugh with joy.
He pledged to me his troth.
Could he forget his oath?
He's forgot what he swore.
Should I say any more?

三岁为妇，靡室劳矣。
夙兴夜寐，靡有朝矣。
言既遂矣，至于暴矣。
兄弟不知，咥其笑矣。
静言思之，躬自悼矣。

及尔偕老，老使我怨。
淇则有岸，隰则有泮。
总角之宴，言笑晏晏，
信誓旦旦，不思其反。
反是不思，亦已焉哉！

My Man's Away

My man's away to serve the state;
I can't anticipate
How long he will there stay
Nor when he'll be on homeward way.
The sun is setting in the west,
The fowls are roosting in their nest,
The sheep and cattle come to rest.
To serve the state my man's away.
How can I not miss him night and day?

My man's away to serve the state;
I can't anticipate
When we'll again have met.
The sun's already set,
The fowls are roosting in their nest,
The sheep and cattle come to rest.
To serve the state my man's away.
Keep him from hunger and thirst, I pray!

君子于役

君子于役，不知其期，
曷至哉？鸡栖于埘，
日之夕矣，羊牛下来。
君子于役，如之何勿思！

君子于役，不日不月，
曷其有佸？鸡栖于桀，
日之夕矣，羊牛下括。
君子于役，苟无饥渴？

Rooster's Crow, Hark!

The wife says, "Rooster's crow, hark!"
The man says, "It's still dark."
"Rise and look at the night;
The morning star shines bright."
"Wild geese and duck will fly;
I'll shoot them down from high."

"At shooting you are good;
I'll dress the game as food.
Together we'll drink wine,
And live to ninety-nine.
With zither by our side,
At peace we shall abide."

"I know your wifely care,
I'll give you pearls to wear.
I know your will to obey.
Can pearls and jade repay?
I know your steadfast love,
I value nothing above."

女曰鸡鸣

女曰“鸡鸣。”士曰“昧旦。”
“子兴视夜，明星有烂。
将翱将翔，弋凫与雁。”

“弋言加之，与子宜之。
宜言饮酒，与子偕老。
琴瑟在御，莫不静好。”

“知子之来之，杂佩以赠之。
知子之顺之，杂佩以问之。
知子之好之，杂佩以报之。”

The Rooster Is Crowing

"Wake up, the rooster is crowing,
The lords to court are going."
"It's not the rooster that cries,
But humming of the flies."

"The east is brightening,
The court is in full swing."
"It's not the east that's bright,
But the moon shedding light."

"The humming insects fly,
It's sweet in bed to lie."
"But lords will leave the hall.
Do not displease them all!"

鸡鸣

“鸡既鸣矣，朝既盈矣。”
“匪鸡则鸣，苍蝇之声。”

“东方明矣，朝既昌矣。”
“匪东方则明，月出之光。”

“虫飞薨薨，甘与子同梦。”
“会且归矣，无庶予子憎。”

Comradeship

Are you not battle-drest?
Let's share the plate for breast.
We shall go up the line.
Let's make our spears and lances shine.
Your foe is mine!

Are you not battle-drest?
Let's share the coat and vest.
We shall go up the line.
Let's make our halberds shine.
Your work is mine!

Are you not battle-drest?
Let's share the kilt, the rest.
We shall go up the line.
Let's make our armor shine.
We'll march in line!

无衣

岂曰无衣？与子同袍。
王于兴师，修我戈矛。
与子同仇！

岂曰无衣？与子同泽。
王于兴师，修我矛戟。
与子偕作！

岂曰无衣？与子同裳。
王于兴师，修我甲兵。
与子偕行！

Homecoming after the War(Excerpt)

When I left here,
Willows shed tear.
Now I come back
On snowy track.
Long, long the way;
Hard, hard the day.
My grief o'erflows.
Who knows? Who knows!

采薇(选段)

昔我往矣，
杨柳依依。
今我来思，
雨雪霏霏。
行道迟迟，
载渴载饥。
我心悲伤，
莫知我哀！

Hunting

Well-built and firm our car,
Well match'd our horses are.
We yoke four horses strong
And eastwards drive along.

Splendid our hunting car;
Sturdy our horses are.
Eastward the grasslands spread;
We drive and hunt ahead.

Our master sallies out,
The picked footmen shout.
With banners they display,
They start to chase the prey.

They drive the four-horsed car.
How strong the horses are!
They're dressed in bright array
As on an audience day.

车攻

我车既攻，我马既同。
四牡庞庞，驾言徂东。

田车既好，四牡孔阜。
东有甫草，驾言行狩。

之子于苗，选徒嚣嚣。
建旐设旄，搏兽于敖。

驾彼四牡，四牡奕奕。
赤芾金舄，会同有绎。

Thimbles and armlets fit;
Arrows from bows will hit.
Together archers shoot;
In piles lie birds and brute.

They drive four horses bay,
No side steeds swerve or sway.
The car straightforward goes;
The arrows fall like blows.

The homing horses neigh,
The footmen flags display.
The archers are so skilled,
With game the kitchen's filled.

Our lord's on homeward way;
He's fairly won the day.
Not words but deeds are good;
In him there's true manhood.

决拾既佽，弓矢既调。
射夫既同，助我举柴。

四黄既驾，两骖不猗。
不失其驰，舍矢如破。

萧萧马鸣，悠悠旆旌。
徒御不惊？大庖不盈？

之子于征，有闻无声。
允矣君子，展也大成！

QU YUAN
(c. 340-c. 278 BC)

To the God of Cloud

Bathed in orchid-scented dews
And dressed in robes of varied hues,
With fleecy hair you slowly rise
To beautify the morning skies.

Within your deathless hall at noon
Your whiteness rivals sun and moon.
The dragon is your charioteer;
You waft and wander far and near.

In silver drops you come with rain;
On wings of wind you rise again.
You gaze upon the land with ease;
You float o'er and beyond Four Seas.
Longing for you, I can't but sigh,
My yearning heart to you would fly.

屈原

（约前 340 – 约前 278）

云中君

浴兰汤兮沐芳，华采衣兮若英。
灵连蜷兮既留，烂昭昭兮未央。
謇将憺兮寿宫，与日月兮齐光。
龙驾兮帝服，聊翱游兮周章。
灵皇皇兮既降，猋远举兮云中。
览冀州兮有余，横四海兮焉穷。
思夫君兮太息，极劳心兮忡忡。

To the Lord of River Xiang

Why don't you come, still hesitating?
For whom on midway isle are you waiting?
Fair and duly adorned, I float
On rapid stream my cassia boat.
I bid the waves more slowly go
And the river tranquilly flow.
I wait for you who have not come;
Playing my flute, with grief I'm numb.

In dragon boat for north I make
And zigzag to Dongting Lake.
Ivy behind, lotus before,
Orchid for flag, cedar for oar,
I gaze on the lake's farthest side;
My soul can't cross the river wide.
Across the river I can't fly;
For my distress my handmaids sigh.
My tears stream down and slowly flow;
Longing for you, I hide my woe.

湘君

君不行兮夷犹，蹇谁留兮中洲？
美要眇兮宜修，沛吾乘兮桂舟。
令沅湘兮无波，使江水兮安流。
望夫君兮未来，吹参差兮谁思？
驾飞龙兮北征，邅吾道兮洞庭。
薜荔柏兮蕙绸，荪桡兮兰旌。
望涔阳兮极浦，横大江兮扬灵。
扬灵兮未极，女婵媛兮为余太息。
横流涕兮潺湲，隐思君兮陫侧。

With orchid rudder and cassia oar,
I break the ice and snow before,
As plucking ivy from the stream
Or lotus from trees in a dream.
The go-between cannot unite
Two divided hearts whose love is light,
As on a shallow stream can't float
Even a winged dragon boat.
Faithless, you are deceiving me;
Breaking our tryst, you say you're not free.

At dawn I drive my cab by riverside;
At eve on northern isle I stop my ride.
Under the eaves the birds repose;
Around the house the river flows.
I throw in water my jade rings
And cast away my offerings.
I pluck sweet flowers on the isle
And give them to maids poor but not vile.
Lost time cannot be found again;
From thinking of you I'd refrain.

桂棹兮兰枻，斫冰兮积雪。
采薜荔兮水中，搴芙蓉兮木末。
心不同兮媒劳，恩不甚兮轻绝。
石濑兮浅浅，飞龙兮翩翩。
交不忠兮怨长，期不信兮告余以不闲！
朝骋骛兮江皋，夕弭节兮北渚。
鸟次兮屋上，水周兮堂下。
捐余玦兮江中，遗余佩兮澧浦。
采芳洲兮杜若，将以遗兮下女。
时不可兮再得，聊逍遥兮容与。

To the Lady of River Xiang

On Northern Isle descends my dear,
But I am grieved to see not clear.
The ceaseless autumn breeze grieves
The Dongting waves with fallen leaves.
I gaze afar 'mid clover white
And wait for our tryst at twilight.
Among the reeds can birds be free?
What can a net do on the tree?
White clover grows beside the creek;
I long for you but dare not speak.
I gaze afar, my beloved one,
I see but rippling water run.
Could deer find food within the door?
What could a dragon do ashore?
At dawn by riverside I urge my steed;
At dusk across the western stream I speed.
For you bid me to come today;
Together we're to ride away.

湘夫人

帝子降兮北渚，目眇眇兮愁予。
袅袅兮秋风，洞庭波兮木叶下。
登白薠兮骋望，与佳期兮夕张。
鸟何萃兮蘋中，罾何为兮木上？
沅有茝兮澧有兰，思公子兮未敢言。
荒忽兮远望，观流水兮潺湲。
麋何食兮庭中，蛟何为兮水裔？
朝驰余马兮江皋，夕济兮西澨。
闻佳人兮召予，将腾驾兮偕逝。

A midstream palace shall be made,
O'er its roof lotus weave a shade.
In purple court thyme decks the wall,
With fragrant pepper spread the hall.
Pillars of cassia stand upright,
And rooms smell sweet with clover white.
We weave the ivy into a screen
And spread the ground with its leaves green.
The cornerstones shall be white jade,
And fragrance of orchids shall not fade.
On lotus roof let vetch be found
And fresh azaleas around.
The courtyard filled with herbs so fair,
The corridor with perfume rare.
All gods will come from mountains high
Like clouds that overspread the sky.

I throw, when waking from my dream,
My shirt with sleeves into the stream.
I pluck sweet flowers on the bay,
I'd give to strangers far away.
Lost time can't oft be found again,
From thinking of you I'd refrain.

筑室兮水中，葺之兮荷盖。
荪壁兮紫坛，播芳椒兮成堂。
桂栋兮兰橑，辛夷楣兮药房。
罔薜荔兮为帷，擗蕙櫋兮既张。
白玉兮为镇，疏石兰兮为芳。
芷葺兮荷屋，缭之兮杜衡。
合百草兮实庭，建芳馨兮庑门。
九嶷缤兮并迎，灵之来兮如云。
捐余袂兮江中，遗余褋兮澧浦。
搴汀洲兮杜若，将以遗兮远者。
时不可兮骤得，聊逍遥兮容与。

For Those Fallen for the Country

We take our southern spears and don our coats of mail;
When chariot axles clash, with daggers we assail.
Banners obscure the sun, the foe roll up like cloud,
Arrows fall thick; forward press our warriors proud.
Our line is broken through, our position o'errun,
My left-hand horse is killed and wounded my right-hand one.
The fallen horses block my wheels and I am stayed;
In vain I beat the sounding drum with rods of jade.
By angry powers' order our men should be slain,
And here and there our warriors' corpses strew the plain.
They came out not to return to where they belong;
The battlefield's so vast, their homeward way so long.
With sword in hand and long bow captured from the west,
Though head and body sever, their heart's not repressed.
They were indeed courageous and ready to fight,
And steadfast to the end, undaunted by armed might.
Their spirit deathless is, although their blood was shed,
Captains among the ghosts, heroes among the dead!

国殇

操吴戈兮被犀甲，车错毂兮短兵接。
旌蔽日兮敌若云，矢交坠兮士争先。
凌余阵兮躐余行，左骖殪兮右刃伤。
霾两轮兮絷四马，援玉枹兮击鸣鼓。
天时怼兮威灵怒，严杀尽兮弃原野。
出不入兮往不反，平原忽兮路超远。
带长剑兮挟秦弓，首身离兮心不惩。
诚既勇兮又以武，终刚强兮不可凌。
身既死兮神以灵，子魂魄兮为鬼雄！

HAN DYNASTY

(206 BC-AD 220)

汉朝

（前 *206*—公元 *220*）

XIANG YU
(232-202 BC)*

The Last Song

I could pull down a mountain with my might,
My fortune wanes and e'en my steed won't fight.
Whether my steed will fight, I do not care.
What can I do with you, my lady fair?

---

* Xiang Yu the conqueror fought against Liu Bang for the throne. Defeated, he and his favorite Lady Yu committed suicide. The lady was so beautiful that her name became a tune title: "The Beautiful Lady Yu."

项羽

（前 232 – 前 202）

垓下歌

力拔山兮气盖世。
时不利兮骓不逝。
骓不逝兮可奈何！
虞兮虞兮奈若何！

LIU BANG
(256-195 BC)*

Song of the Big Wind

A big wind rises, clouds are driven away.
Home am I now the world is under my sway.
Where are brave men to guard the four frontiers today?

* First emperor of the Han Dynasty (256-195 BC).

刘邦

（前 256 – 前 195）

大风歌

大风起兮云飞扬，
威加海内兮归故乡。
安得猛士兮守四方！

NINETEEN OLD POEMS

You Travel On and On

You travel on and on
And leave me all alone.
Away ten thousand li,
At the end of the sea.
Severed by hard, long way,
Oh, can we meet someday?
Northern steeds love cold breeze,
And southern birds warm trees.
The farther you are away,
The thinner I am each day.
The cloud has veiled the sun;
You won't come back, dear one.
Missing you makes me old;
Soon comes the winter cold.
Alas! Of me you're quit.
I hope you will keep fit.

古诗十九首

行行重行行

行行重行行，与君生别离。
相去万余里，各在天一涯。
道路阻且长，会面安可知！
胡马依北风，越鸟巢南枝。
相去日已远，衣带日已缓。
浮云蔽白日，游子不顾返。
思君令人老，岁月忽已晚。
弃捐勿复道，努力加餐饭！

FOLK SONGS

The Roadside Mulberry

The rising sun from southeast nook
Shines on the house of Qin, who
Has a daughter of lovely looks;
She calls herself Luo-fu.
She picks mulberry leaves still new
To feed silkworms in southern nook,
Her basket's bound with silk thread blue,
Of laurel bough is made a hook.
Her hair is dressed in pretty braid,
Like moonbeams her pearl earrings shine,
Of yellow silk her apron's made,
Her cloak of purple damask fine.

When she is seen by passers-by,
They stroke their beards and there take root;
When she appears in young men's eye,
They doff their caps and make salute.
The ploughman thinks not of his plough,
The hoer leaves in field his hoe.
Back, they find fault with their wives now,
For they have seen Luo-fu aglow.
From the south comes the governor,
Whose carriage and five stop and stay.
He sends men to inquire of her.
"Who are you, pretty maid?" ask they.

乐府

陌上桑

日出东南隅，照我秦氏楼。
秦氏有好女，自名为罗敷。
罗敷喜蚕桑，采桑城南隅。
青丝为笼系，桂枝为笼钩。
头上倭堕髻，耳中明月珠。
缃绮为下裙，紫绮为上襦。

行者见罗敷，下担捋髭须。
少年见罗敷，脱帽著帩头。
耕者忘其犁，锄者忘其锄。
来归相怨怒，但坐观罗敷。

使君从南来，五马立踟蹰。
使君遣吏往，问是谁家姝？

"I call my humble self Luo-fu."
"Pretty Luo-fu, how old are you?"
"My age is still less than a score,
But much more than fifteen, much more."
"We are bid by our lord, oh, pretty Luo-fu,
To ask if riding with him would please you."

Luo-fu steps forth and makes reply:
"What nonsense you are talking. Why,
Your Excellency has his wife;
I have my husband dear for life.
There are more than a thousand steeds
In the east that my husband leads."

"But how can I your husband know?"
"Ah, by his horse as white as snow,
Whose tail is tied with a blue thread,
With golden halters round its head;
By the sword with its hilt of jade,
For which its weight in gold he paid.

"At fifteen he was a junior clerk;
At twenty he did a courtier's work;
At thirty he wore chamberlain's gown;
At forty he was lord of a town.

"His face and skin are white and fair,
A rather long beard he does wear.
In the court he walks to and fro,
And goes to the palace with steps slow.
Among the thousands in the hall,
He's deemed the most distinguished of all."

“秦氏有好女，自名为罗敷。”
“罗敷年几何？”
“二十尚不足，十五颇有余。”
“使君谢罗敷，宁可共载不？”

罗敷前置辞：“使君一何愚！
使君自有妇，罗敷自有夫。”
“东方千余骑，夫婿居上头。

何用识夫婿？白马从骊驹。
青丝系马尾，黄金络马头。
腰中鹿卢剑，可值千万余。

十五府小吏，二十朝大夫，
三十侍中郎，四十专城居。

为人洁白晰，鬑鬑颇有须。
盈盈公府步，冉冉府中趋。
坐中数千人，皆言夫婿殊。”

LIU CHE (156-87 BC) *

Song of the Autumn Wind

The autumn wind rises and white clouds fly,
When leaves turn yellow, wild geese head for southern sky.
The orchids and chrysanthemums still sweeten the air.
Oh, how can I forget my lady sweet and fair!
I go aboard a bark to cross the river long;
It reaches midstream when I see the waves rise white.
The flutes and drums keep time to the rowers' song,
But sorrow comes when pleasure reaches its height.
How long will youth endure when old age is in sight!

* Emperor Wu of the Han Dynasty, who wrote the elegy for his favorite Lady Li.

刘彻

（前 156 – 前 87）

秋风辞

秋风起兮白云飞，草木黄落兮雁南归。
兰有秀兮菊有芳，怀佳人兮不能忘。
泛楼船兮济汾河，横中流兮扬素波。
箫鼓鸣兮发棹歌，欢乐极兮哀情多。
少壮几时兮奈老何！

LADY BAN
(Dates Unknown)*

Lament of the Autumn Fan

Fresh from the weaver's loom, O silk so white,
As clear as frost, as winter snow as bright.
Fashioned into a fan, token of love,
You are as round as brilliant moon above.
In my lord's sleeve when in or out he goes,
You wave and shake and a light wind blows.
I fear when comes the autumn day,
And chilling wind drives summer heat away,
You'll be discarded to a lonely place,
And with my lord fall into disgrace.

* The favorite of Emperor Cheng of the Han Dynasty, who fell into disgrace like the autumn fan, which has become a symbol of disgrace since then.

班婕妤

（生卒年不详）

怨歌行

新裂齐纨素，鲜洁如霜雪。
裁为合欢扇，团团似明月。
出入君怀袖，动摇微风发。
常恐秋节至，凉飙夺炎热。
弃捐箧笥中，恩情中道绝。

CAO CAO
(155-220) *

The Sea

I come to view the boundless ocean
From Stony Hill on eastern shore.
Its water rolls in rhythmic motion,
And islands stand amid its roar.

Tree on tree grows from peak to peak;
Grass on grass looks lush far and nigh.
The autumn wind blows drear and bleak;
The monstrous billows surge up high.

The sun by day, the moon by night
Appear to rise up from the deep.
The Milky Way with stars so bright
Sinks down into the sea in sleep.

How happy I feel at this sight!
I croon this poem in delight.

* Sovereign of the Kingdom of Wei.

曹操

（155–220）

观沧海

东临碣石，以观沧海。
水何澹澹，山岛竦峙。
树木丛生，百草丰茂。
秋风萧瑟，洪波涌起。
日月之行，若出其中；
星汉灿烂，若出其里。
幸甚至哉，歌以咏志。

CAO PI
(186-226)

On the Death of My Father*

Raising my eyes, I see his screen;
Bending my head, his table clean.
These things are there just as before,
The man who owned them is no more.
Suddenly his spirit has flown
And left me fatherless, alone.
Who'd look to me? On whom rely?
Tear upon tear streams from my eye.
The deer are bleating here and there,
They feed the young ones in their care.
The birds are flying east and west,
Feeding the nestlings in the nest.
Alone I'm desolate and drear,
Severed from the father I revere.
Deep in my heart grief overflows,
But no one knows, no one knows.
'Tis said that sorrow makes us old
And early grow white hair. Behold!
For the deceased I wail and sigh;
If the good live long, why should he die!

* Cao Cao (155-220), King of Wei.

曹丕
（186–226）

短歌行

仰瞻帷幕，俯察几筵。
其物如故，其人不存。
神灵倏忽，弃我遐迁。
靡瞻靡恃，泣涕涟涟。
呦呦游鹿，衔草鸣麑。
翩翩飞鸟，挟子巢栖。
我独孤茕，怀此百离。
忧心孔疚，莫我能知！
人亦有言，“忧令人老”。
嗟我白发，生一何早！
长吟永叹，怀我圣考。
曰“仁者寿”，胡不是保？

CAO ZHI
(192-232)*

Written While Taking Seven Paces

Pods burned to cook peas,
Peas weep in the pot:
Grown from the same trees,
Why boil us so hot?

* Cao Zhi was the younger brother of Cao Pi who, after coming to the throne, ordered him to compose a poem while taking seven paces and he wrote this quatrain in which pods and peas allude to brothers at odds.

曹植
（192–232）

七步诗

煮豆燃豆萁，
豆在釜中泣。
本是同根生，
相煎何太急。

ANONYMOUS

A Pair of Peacocks Southeast Fly

During the reign of Jian'an (196-219) in the Eastern Han Dynasty there was a local official in the prefecture of Lujiang called Jiao Zhongqing, whose wife, LiuLanzhi, was sent away by his mother and vowed never to marry again. Compelled by her family to break her vow, she had no recourse but to drown herself in a pool. On hearing the news, Zhongqing hanged himself on a tree in the courtyard. The following poem was composed by contemporaries in their memory.

A pair of peacocks southeast fly;
At each mile they look back and cry.

"I could weave," said Lanzhi, "at thirteen
And learned to cut clothes at fourteen;
At fifteen to play music light;
At sixteen to read and to write.
At seventeen to you I was wed.
What an austere life I have led!
"You're an official far away;
I toil as housewife night and day.
At daybreak I begin to weave;
At night the loom I dare not leave.
I've finished five rolls in three days,
Yet I am blamed for my delays.
Not that my work is done too slow,
But hard your housewife's role does grow.

无名氏

孔雀东南飞

汉末建安中，庐江府小吏焦仲卿妻刘氏，为仲卿母所遣，自誓不嫁。其家逼之，乃投水而死。仲卿闻之，亦自缢于庭树。时人伤之，为诗云尔。

孔雀东南飞，五里一徘徊。
“十三能织素，十四学裁衣，
十五弹箜篌，十六诵诗书。
十七为君妇，心中常苦悲。
君既为府吏，守节情不移。
贱妾留空房，相见常日稀。
鸡鸣入机织，夜夜不得息。
三日断五匹，大人故嫌迟。
非为织作迟，君家妇难为。

If Mother thinks I am no good,
What use to stay, although I would?
Will you come and to Mother say,
Send me back home without delay?"

Jiao Zhongqing came home at her call
And said to his mother in the hall,
"I'm destined for a humble life;
By fortune I have this good wife.
We've shared the pillow, mat and bed,
And we'll be man and wife till dead.
We've lived together but three years,
Which not too long to me appears.
She has done nothing wrong, I find.
Why should you be to her unkind?"

His mother said then in reply,
"You are indeed shortsighted. Why,
This wife of yours with me goes ill;
She always does whate'er she will.
I've been offended by her for long.
How dare you say she's done no wrong?
In the east there's a match for you,
A maiden whose name's Qin Luo-fu,
A peerless beauty of this land.
I'll go for you to ask her hand.
Now send your slut out of our door!
She should not stay here anymore."

Zhongqing knelt down with trunk erect
And said to her with due respect,
"If you should send away my wife,
I won't remarry all my life."

妾不堪驱使，徒留无所施。
便可白公姥，及时相遣归。”
府吏得闻之，堂上启阿母：
“儿已薄禄相，幸复得此妇。
结发同枕席，黄泉共为友。
共事二三年，始尔未为久。
女行无偏斜，何意致不厚？”
阿母谓府吏：“何乃太区区！
此妇无礼节，举动自专由。
吾意久怀忿，汝岂得自由！
东家有贤女，自名秦罗敷。
可怜体无比，阿母为汝求。
便可速遣之，遣去慎莫留！”
府吏长跪告，伏惟启阿母：
“今若遣此妇,终老不复取！”

The mother was angry at his word;
Her strumming on the stool was heard.
"Has filial reverence come to nil?
Defend your wife against my will!
You are such an ungrateful son!
Of your request I will grant none."

Zhongqing dared not speak any more,
But bowed and entered his own door.
He tells his wife when she appears,
His voice choked so with bitter tears,
"Not that I would send you away,
But Mother won't allow you to stay.
Return to your brother's house, so
That to my office I may go.
When I have finished my work, then
I'll come and fetch you home again.
Do not be grieved to say adieu,
But keep in mind what I've told you!"

"Nay, make no care to come for me!"
To her husband addresses she.
"One early spring day, I recall,'
I left home for your entrance hall.
I've done what Mother ordered me.
Dare I be careless and carefree?
I do hard labor day and night;
Alone I toil with all my might.

阿母得闻之，槌床便大怒：
“小子无所畏，何敢助妇语！
吾已失恩义，会不相从许！”

府吏默无声，再拜还入户。
举言谓新妇，哽咽不能语：
“我自不驱卿，逼迫有阿母。
卿但暂还家，吾今且报府。
不久当归还，还必相迎取。
以此下心意，慎勿违吾语。”
新妇谓府吏：“勿复重纷纭！
往昔初阳岁，谢家来贵门，
奉事循公姥，进止敢自专？
昼夜勤作息，伶俜萦苦辛。
谓言无罪过，供养卒大恩。
仍更被驱遣，何言复来还？

I think I have done nothing wrong,
Still with Mother I can't get along.
To what avail to talk about
Returning now I'm driven out!

"I'll leave my jacket of brocade,
Whose lacings bright of gold are made,
And my canopy of gauze red,
Whose four corners with perfume spread,
And sixty trunks and coffers tied
With silken threads all in green dyed,
Where different things you will find;
Not two of them are of a kind.
They are as cheap as I, it's true,
Not good enough for your spouse new.
So as gifts you may share them out,
As we can't meet again, no doubt.
Keep them in memory of me!
Forgetful we can never be."

At dawn she rose at the cockcrow
And made up with care, ready to go.
She put on an embroidered gown
And checked it over, up and down.
She put on shoes made of brocade,
Of tortoise shell her hairpin's made.
Her waist was girt with girdle white,
Her earrings shone like moonlight bright.
She had tapering finger tips,
Like rubies were her rouged lips.
She moved at slow and easy pace,
Unrivalled in the human race.

妾有绣腰襦，葳蕤自生光。
红罗复斗帐，四角垂香囊。
箱帘六七十，绿碧青丝绳，
物物各自异，种种在其中。
人贱物亦鄙，不足迎后人，
留待作遗施，于今无会因。
时时为安慰，久久莫相忘。”

鸡鸣外欲曙，新妇起严妆。
著我绣夹裙，事事四五通：
足下蹑丝履，头上玳瑁光。
腰若流纨素，耳著明月珰。
指如削葱根，口如含朱丹。
纤纤作细步，精妙世无双。

She came to his mother in the hall,
Who said no tender words at all.
"While young, before I was a spouse,
I lived but in a country house.
Not well instructed or wide read,
For noble heir I was ill-bred.
Though kindly you have treated me,
Yet I'm not dutiful," said she,
"So I must go back in despair,
Leaving to you all household care."

She said to his sister good-bye;
Bitter tears trickled from her eye.
"When your brother and I were wed,
You came around our nuptial bed.
You are as tall as I today,
When I am to be driven away.
Take good care of your mother old,
And take good care of your household!
When maidens hold their festive day,
Do not forget me while you play."
She went out and got on the cart;
Tears streamed down, heavy was her heart.

Jiao Zhongqing rides before, his mind
Turning to his wife's cart behind.
The cart's rumble's heard to repeat,
The husband stops where four roads meet.
He gets down from his horse, comes near
His wife and whispers in her ear,
"I swear not to leave you long, my spouse.
Return now to your brother's house.

上堂拜阿母，阿母怒不止。
“昔作女儿时，生小出野里。
本自无教训，兼愧贵家子。
受母钱帛多，不堪母驱使。
今日还家去，念母劳家里。”
却与小姑别，泪落连珠子。
“新妇初来时，小姑始扶床；
今日被驱遣，小姑如我长。
勤心养公姥，好自相扶将。
初七及下九，嬉戏莫相忘。”
出门登车去，涕落百余行。

府吏马在前，新妇车在后。
隐隐何甸甸，俱会大道口。
下马入车中，低头共耳语：
“誓不相隔卿，且暂还家去。

When I have finished my work, then
I'll come and fetch you home again.
I swear to heaven high above
That forever will last our love."
Lanzhi says to her husband dear,
"I'm touched by your love sincere.
If I'm engraved deep in your mind,
Come then in time and not behind!
If as the rock your love is strong,
Then mine as creeping vine is long.
The vine's resistant as silk thread;
No one could lift a rock o'erhead.
But my brother's temper is hot,
Look on me kindly he will not.
I am afraid he'll never care
What I like, and it's hard to bear."
They wave their hands with broken heart,
From each other they will not part.

Lanzhi came to her mother's place,
Feeling embarrassed in disgrace.
Her mother clapped loud in surprise:
"How can you come back in this guise!
You were taught to weave at thirteen;
To cut the clothes at fourteen;
At fifteen to play music light;
At sixteen to perform the rite.
At seventeen you were a bride;
By your husband you should abide.
Had you done nothing wrong at all,
Why come back alone to my hall?"
Lanzhi told her mother the truth,
Who was moved to tears, full of ruth.

吾今且赴府，不久当还归。
誓天不相负！”
新妇谓府吏：“感君区区怀！
君既若见录，不久望君来。
君当作磐石，妾当作蒲苇。
蒲苇纫如丝，磐石无转移。
我有亲父兄，性行暴如雷，
恐不任我意，逆以煎我怀。”
举手长劳劳，二情同依依 。

入门上家堂，进退无颜仪。
阿母大拊掌：“不图子自归！
十三教汝织，十四能裁衣，
十五弹箜篌，十六知礼仪，
十七遣汝嫁，谓言无誓违。
汝今何罪过，不迎而自归？”
兰芝惭阿母：“儿实无罪过。”
阿母大悲摧。

She had been back many a day,
A go-between then came to say,
"Our magistrate has a third son,
Whose good looks are second to none.
Though at eighteen or nineteen years,
For eloquence he has no peers."
Her mother said to her, "Consent
To this proposal benevolent!"
But she only answered in tears,
"Can I forget my married years?
My husband vowed when we parted then,
Never should we sever again.
If I should break my word today,
I would regret for e'er and aye.
Will you please tell the go-between
Gently and clearly what I mean?"
Her mother told the messenger,
"This humble daughter of mine, sir,
Sent back by an official of late,
Can't match a son of magistrate.
Why not inquire another house
Where may be found a better spouse?"

还家十余日，县令遣媒来。
云“有第三郎，窈窕世无双，
年始十八九，便言多令才。”
阿母谓阿女：“汝可去应之。”
阿女含泪答：“兰芝初还时，
府吏见丁宁，结誓不别离。
今日违情义，恐此事非奇。
自可断来信，徐徐更谓之。”
阿母白媒人：“贫贱有此女，
始适还家门。不堪吏人妇，
岂合令郎君？幸可广问讯，
不得便相许。”

No sooner had gone this messenger
Than came one from the governor.
"You have a daughter fair," said he,
"Of an official's family.
Our governor has a fifth son,
Unmarried, he's a handsome one.
My lord's secretary asked me
His lordship's go-between to be.
I was told to say openly
I come for my lord's family.
His son will have your daughter for spouse.
That's why I'm sent to your noble house."

Mother Liu thanked the messenger,
But said she could not order her
Who'd made a vow, to break her word.
By Lanzhi's brother this was heard;
As it troubled his worldly mind,
He spoke to Lanzhi words unkind.
"Why don't you, sister, think it o'er?
You left then an official's door;
Now you may marry a noble son;
Good luck comes when bad luck is done.
If you refuse this honor great,
I know not what will be your fate."

Lanzhi replied, raising her head,
"Brother, it's right what you have said.
I left you once to be a spouse;
Sent back, again I'm in your house.
So I'm at your disposal now.
Can I do what you don't allow?

媒人去数日，寻遣丞请还，
说“有兰家女，承籍有宦官。”
云“有第五郎，娇逸未有婚。
遣丞为媒人，主簿通语言。”
直说“太守家，有此令郎君，
既欲结大义，故遣来贵门。”
阿母谢媒人：“女子先有誓，
老姥岂敢言！”阿兄得闻之，
怅然心中烦。举言谓阿妹：
“作计何不量！先嫁得府吏，
后嫁得郎君。否泰如天地，
足以荣汝身。不嫁义郎体，
其往欲何云？”兰芝仰头答：
“理实如兄言。谢家事夫婿，
中道还兄门。处分适兄意，
那得自任专！

Though I vowed to my husband dear,
We cannot meet again, I fear.
So you may marry me at will,
My obligation I'll fulfil."

The go-between learned what they said,
To his lord's house he went ahead.
He said his errand was well done;
The lord rejoiced for his fifth son.
He found in the almanac soon
The auspicious date of that moon.
He said to his subordinate,
"The thirtieth day is the best date.
That is only three days ahead.
Arrange the marriage in my stead."

The lord's order was given loud;
People bustled like floating cloud.
They painted with bird designs the boat
And with dragons the flags afloat.
A golden cab with wheels trimmed with jade
And golden saddles for steeds were made.
Three thousand strings of coins were sent
And silks to the bride with compliment.
Delicacies from land and sea
Were brought by two corteges or three.

虽与府吏要，渠会永无缘。
登即相许和，便可作婚姻。”
媒人下床去，诺诺复尔尔。

还部白府君：
“下官奉使命，言谈大有缘。”
府君得闻之，心中大欢喜。
视历复开书，便利此月内，
六合正相应。“良吉三十日，
今已二十七，卿可去成婚。”
交语速装束，络绎如浮云。
青雀白鹄舫，四角龙子幡。
婀娜随风转，金车玉作轮。
踯躅青骢马，流苏金镂鞍。
赍钱三百万，皆用青丝穿。
杂彩三百匹，交广市鲑珍。
从人四五百，郁郁登郡门。

Mother Liu told her daughter, "Word
Comes from the governor have you heard?
Tomorrow is your wedding day.
Put yourself in bridal array.
Make your own dress ere it's too late!"
Lanzhi sat in a pensive state.
She sobbed 'neath her handkerchief,
And streaming tears revealed her grief.
She dragged a marble-seated chair
Towards the window in despair,
In her left hand the scissors bright
And silk and satin in her right.
At noon a jacket new was made
And at dusk a robe in brocade.
Behind dark clouds the sun down crept,
Grief-stricken, she went out and wept.

Zhongqing, at this news of his spouse,
Asks leave and starts out for her house.
After a short ride on his way,
His horse makes an anguished neigh.
This neigh is familiar to her ears;
She comes out before he appears.
She gazes afar, at a loss
What to say when he comes across.
She pats the horse when it comes nigh,
And then says with a woeful sigh,
"Alas! Since you parted with me,
What's happened we could not foresee,

阿母谓阿女："适得府君书，
明日来迎汝。何不作衣裳？
莫令事不举！"阿女默无声，
手巾掩口啼，泪落便如泻。
移我琉璃榻，出置前窗下。
左手持刀尺，右手执绫罗。
朝成绣夹裙，晚成单罗衫。
晻晻日欲暝，愁思出门啼。

府吏闻此变，因求假暂归。
未至二三里，摧藏马悲哀。
新妇识马声，蹑履相逢迎。
怅然遥相望，知是故人来。
举手拍马鞍，嗟叹使心伤：
"自君别我后，人事不可量。

Our hope cannot be realized.
On hearing this, you'll be surprised.
I was compelled by my own mother
Together with my tyrant brother
To wed another man at last.
What can we do? The die is cast."
Jiao Zhongqing tells his former wife,
"I wish you a happier life!
The lofty rock steadfast appears;
It will stand for thousands of years.
Howe'er resistant the vine may be,
'Twill lose its toughness easily.
May you live happier day by day!
Alone to death I'll go my way."
"Why say such cruel things to me?"
To her former husband says she,
"We are compelled, both you and I.
How could I live if you should die?
E'en dead, let us together stay!
Forget not what we've said today!"
They stand long hand in hand before
They go each to his or her door.
No lovers know a sharper pain
Than to part till death joins them again.
They're willing to breathe their last breath;
A severed life is worse than death.

Jiao Zhongqing went home full of gloom;
He went straight to his mother's room.
"Today the cold wind blows down trees;
Bitten by frost, the orchids freeze.

果不如先愿，又非君所详。
我有亲父母，逼迫兼弟兄。
以我应他人，君还何所望！”
府吏谓新妇：“贺卿得高迁！
磐石方且厚，可以卒千年；
蒲苇一时纫，便作旦夕间。
卿当日胜贵，吾独向黄泉！”
新妇谓府吏：“何意出此言！
同是被逼迫，君尔妾亦然。
黄泉下相见，勿违今日言！”
执手分道去，各各还家门。
生人作死别，恨恨那可论！
念与世间辞，千万不复全。

府吏还家去，上堂拜阿母：
“今日大风寒，寒风摧树木，
严霜结庭兰。

I fear my life will end like the tree,
Leaving you alone after me.
That's what such forebodings proclaim.
Don't lay on gods or ghosts the blame!
May you like hillside rock live long
With your four limbs both straight and strong!"

On hearing this, his mother shed
Copious tears before she said,
"As son of noble family,
A high official you should be.
How could you die for such a wife?
Don't play down on your noble life!
There's a maiden in east neighbourhood,
Beside her no one else is good.
I have wooed her to be your spouse;
Soon the reply will come to our house."
Zhongqing retired to his empty room,
Determined not to be a bridegroom.
He sighed and glanced towards the hall,
Seeing his tragic curtain fall.

In the blue tent on her wedding day
Lanzhi heard cows low and steeds neigh.
At dusk the ghostly twilight waned;
The guests gone, lonely she remained.
"My life," she thought, "will end today.
My soul will go, but my body stay."
She doffed her silken shoes to drown
Herself in uprolled wedding gown.

儿今日冥冥，令母在后单。
故作不良计，勿复怨鬼神！
命如南山石，四体康且直！”

阿母得闻之，零泪应声落：
“汝是大家子，仕宦于台阁。
慎勿为妇死，贵贱情何薄！
东家有贤女，窈窕艳城郭，
阿母为汝求，便复在旦夕。”
府吏再拜还，长叹空房中，
作计乃尔立。转头向户里，
渐见愁煎迫。

其日牛马嘶，新妇入青庐。
奄奄黄昏后，寂寂人定初。
我命绝今日，魂去尸长留！
揽裙脱丝履，举身赴清池。

This news came to her Zhongqing's ear;
He would not be severed from his dear.
To and fro in the yard paced he,
Then hanged himself beneath a tree.

Their families, after they died,
Buried them by the mountainside.
Pine trees were planted left and right,
And planes and cypresses on the site.
Their foliage darkens the ground;
Their branches intertwined are found.
A pair of peacocks fly above;
They are well known as birds of love.
Heads up, they sing song after song,
From night to night, and all night long.
A passer-by would stand spellbound;
A lonely widow would wake dumfound.

Men of posterity, I pray,
Do not forget that bygone day!

府吏闻此事，心知长别离。
徘徊庭树下，自挂东南枝。

两家求合葬，合葬华山傍。
东西植松柏，左右种梧桐。
枝枝相覆盖，叶叶相交通。
中有双飞鸟，自名为鸳鸯。
仰头相向鸣，夜夜达五更。
行人驻足听，寡妇起彷徨。
多谢后世人，戒之慎勿忘。

SIX DYNASTIES

(222-589)

六朝

（222—589）

TAO QIAN
(c. 365-427)

Return to Nature (I)

While young, I was not used to worldly cares,
And hills became my natural compeers,
But by mistake I fell in mundane snares
And thus entangled was for thirteen years.
A caged bird would long for wonted wood,
And fish in tanks for native pools would yearn.
Go back to till my southern fields I would
To live a rustic life why not return?
My plot of ground is but ten acres square;
My thatched cottage has eight or nine rooms.
In front I have peach trees here and plums there;
O'er back eaves willow trees and elms cast glooms.
A village can be seen in distant dark,
Where plumes of smoke rise and waft in the breeze.
In alley deep a dog is heard to bark,
And cocks crow as if o'er mulberry trees.
Into my courtyard no one should intrude,
Nor rob my private rooms of peace and leisure.
After long years of abject servitude,
Again in nature I find homely pleasure.

陶潜

（约 365–427）

归园田居（其一）

少无适俗韵，性本爱丘山。
误落尘网中，一去三十年。
羁鸟恋旧林，池鱼思故渊。
开荒南野际，守拙归园田。
方宅十余亩，草屋八九间。
榆柳荫后檐，桃李罗堂前。
暧暧远人村，依依墟里烟。
狗吠深巷中，鸡鸣桑树颠。
户庭无尘杂，虚室有余闲。
久在樊笼里，复得返自然。

Drinking Wine

Among the haunts of men I build my cot,
There's noise of wheels and hoofs, but I hear not.
How can it leave upon my mind no trace?
Secluded heart creates secluded place.
I pick fence-side chrysanthemums at will
And leisurely I see the southern hill,
Where mountain air is fresh both day and night,
And where I find home-going birds in flight.
What is the revelation at this view?
Words fail me e'en if I try to tell you.

饮酒

结庐在人境，而无车马喧。
问君何能尔？心远地自偏。
采菊东篱下，悠然见南山。
山气日夕佳，飞鸟相与还。
此中有真意，欲辩已忘言。

An Elegy for Myself (I)

Wherever there is life, there must be death;
Sooner or later we'll breathe our last breath.
Last night we lived as men who fill their posts;
Today my name's enlisted among the ghosts.
Where is my soul that's fled far, far away?
A shriveled form in wooden box would stay.
My children seek after their father, crying;
My friends caress my dead body, sighing.
For gain or loss I no longer care,
And right or wrong is no more my affair.
Thousands of springs and autumns pass away,
So will disgrace and glory of today.
Perchance I may regret, while living still,
I have not drunken good wine to my fill.

拟挽歌辞（其一）

有生必有死，早终非命促。
昨暮同为人，今旦在鬼录。
魂气散何之，枯形寄空木。
娇儿索父啼，良友抚我哭。
得失不复知，是非安能觉。
千秋万岁后，谁知荣与辱。
但恨在世时，饮酒不得足。

BAO ZHAO
(c. 414-466)

The Mume

In midcourt there are many trees,
To the mume my admiration goes.
Why this singular favor, please?*
In defiance of frost it blows.
It has borne fruit in spite of frost
And danced in wind to win the vernal morn,
While other blooms in icy blasts are lost
Or from the branches they are torn.

* Weng Xianliang's translation versified.

鲍照
（约 414–466）

梅花落

中庭多杂树，
偏为梅咨嗟。
“问君何独然？”
“念其霜中能作花，
露中能作实。
摇荡春风媚春日，
念尔零落逐寒风，
徒有霜华无霜质！”

XIE TIAO
(464-499)

Ascending the Three Peaks at Dusk and Gazing at the Capital

Like poets of bygone days
Fixing on the capital their gaze,
I see from distance high and low
Winglike tiled roofs in sunset's glow.
The colored clouds spread like brocade,
The river calm as silver braid.
The islet's loud with birds' wild cries,
Fragrant with blooms of varied dyes.
Oh, I am going far away.
Can I not miss this merry day?
When may I come and stay again?
Tears fall like pearls of snow or rain.
So deeply I long to be back
My hair turns grey from black.

谢朓

（464–499）

晚登三山还望京邑

灞涘望长安，河阳视京县。
白日丽飞甍，参差皆可见。
余霞散成绮，澄江静如练。
喧鸟覆春洲，杂英满芳甸。
去矣方滞淫，怀哉罢欢宴。
佳期怅何许，泪下如流霰。
有情知望乡，谁能鬒不变？

WEI DING
(c. 515-593)

To a Blackbird at the Capital

Scenes change when we are far apart;
A burst of song strikes me to the heart.
How could you sing to those who roam
The tune they used to hear at home!*

* Weng Xianliang's translation versified.

韦鼎

（约 515–593）

长安听百舌

万里风烟异，
一鸟忽相惊。
那能对远客，
还作故乡声？

ANONYMOUS

A Shepherd's Song

By the side of the rill,
At the foot of the hill,
The grassland stretches 'neath the firmament tranquil.

The boundless grassland lies
Beneath the boundless skies.
When the winds blow
And grass bends low,
My sheep and cattle will emerge before your eyes.

无名氏

敕勒歌

敕勒川，
阴山下。
天似穹庐，
笼盖四野。
天苍苍，
野茫茫。
风吹草低见牛羊。

Song of the Western Islet

Dreaming of the mume blossoms snowing,
To Western Islet again she's going;
She'll send a sprig to northern shore
For her beloved she sees no more.
In apricot-yellow silk dress,
E'en blackbirds envy her dark tress.
Where is the Western Islet? Where?
She rows across the bridge o'er there,
Only to find shrikes wheeling low*
And through the trees at dusk winds blow.

Beneath the tree, inside the gate,
Her hair adorned, she comes to wait.
Her lover comes not to her bower;
She goes to gather lotus flower.
In south pool she plucks lotus red,
Which grows e'en high above her head.
She bows and picks some lotus seed
So green that water can't exceed.

西洲曲

忆梅下西洲，折梅寄江北。
单衫杏子红，双鬓鸦雏色。
西洲在何处？两桨桥头渡。
日暮伯劳飞，风吹乌臼树。
树下即门前，门中露翠钿。
开门郎不至，出门采红莲。
采莲南塘秋，莲花过人头。
低头弄莲子，莲子清如水。

She puts some flowers in her sleeves,
Red at the core as she perceives.
He still comes not; she's ill at ease
And watches for flying wild geese.
The geese are mute just as the flower;
She goes to the top of the tower.
To bring him within sight it fails;*
All day long she stops at the rails.
In vain she leans on balustrade,
Lets fall her hands, white like jade.
She sees as she rolls up the screen
The sky and waves in vain are green.

"Our dreams are severed by the sea,
From grief nor you nor I am free.
If the south wind should know my heart,
It would not set us far apart."

---

* Weng Xianliang's translation versified.

置莲怀袖中，莲心彻底红。
忆郎郎不至，仰首望飞鸿。
鸿飞满西洲，望郎上青楼。
楼高望不见，尽日栏杆头。
栏杆十二曲，垂手明如玉。
卷帘天自高，海水摇空绿。
海水梦悠悠，君愁我亦愁。
南风知我意，吹梦到西洲。

Song of Mulan

Alack, alas! Alack, alas!*
She weaves and sees the shuttle pass.
You cannot hear the shuttle, why?
Its whir is drowned in her deep sigh.

"Oh, what are you thinking about?
Will you tell us? Will you speak out?"
"I have no worry on my mind,
Nor have I grief of any kind.
I read the battle roll last night;
The Khan has ordered men to fight.
The roll was written in twelve books;
My father's name was in twelve nooks.
My father has no grown-up son,
For elder brother I have none.
I'll get a horse of hardy race
And serve in my old father's place."

She buys a steed at eastern fair,
A whip and saddle here or there.
She buys a bridle at the south
And metal bit for horse's mouth.

木兰诗

唧唧复唧唧，木兰当户织。
不闻机杼声，唯闻女叹息。
“问女何所思，问女何所忆？”
“女亦无所思，女亦无所忆。
昨夜见军帖，可汗大点兵，
军书十二卷，卷卷有爷名。
阿爷无大儿，木兰无长兄，
愿为市鞍马，从此替爷征。”

东市买骏马，西市买鞍鞯，
南市买辔头，北市买长鞭。

At dawn she leaves her parents by the city wall;
At dusk she reaches Yellow River shore.
All night she listens for old folks' familiar call,
But hears only the Yellow River's roar.

At dawn she leaves the Yellow River shore;
To Mountains Black she goes her way.
At night she hears old folks' familiar voice no more,
But only on north mountains Tatar horses neigh.

For miles and miles the army march along
And cross the mountain barriers as in flight.
The northern wind has chilled the watchman's gong,
Their coat of mail glistens in wintry light.
In ten years they've lost many captains strong,
But battle-hardened warriors come back in delight.

Back, they have their audience with the Khan in the hall,
Honors and gifts are lavished on warriors all.
The Khan asks her what she wants as a grace.
"A camel fleet to carry me to my native place."

Hearing that she has come,
Her parents hurry to meet her at city gate,
Her sister rouges her face at home,
Her younger brother kills pig and sheep to celebrate.

旦辞爷娘去，暮宿黄河边，
不闻爷娘唤女声，但闻黄河流水鸣溅溅。
旦辞黄河去，暮至黑山头，
不闻爷娘唤女声，但闻燕山胡骑鸣啾啾。

万里赴戎机，关山度若飞。
朔气传金柝，寒光照铁衣。
将军百战死，壮士十年归。

归来见天子，天子坐明堂。
策勋十二转，赏赐百千强。
可汗问所欲，“木兰不用尚书郎，
愿驰千里足，送儿还故乡。”

爷娘闻女来，出郭相扶将；
阿姊闻妹来，当户理红妆；
小弟闻姊来，磨刀霍霍向猪羊。

She opens the doors east and west
And sits on her bed for a rest.
She doffs her garb worn under fire
And wears again female attire.
Before the window she arranges her hair
And in the mirror sees her image fair.
Then she comes out to see her former mate,
Who stares at her in amazement great:
"We have marched together for twelve years,
We did not know there was a lass 'mid our compeers!"
"Both buck and doe have a lilting gait
And both their eyelids palpitate.
When side by side two rabbits go,
Who can tell the buck from the doe?"*

* Weng Xianliang's translation versified.

开我东阁门，坐我西阁床。
脱我战时袍，著我旧时裳。
当窗理云鬓，对镜贴花黄。
出门看火伴，火伴皆惊忙：
“同行十二年，不知木兰是女郎。”

“雄兔脚扑朔，雌兔眼迷离，
双兔傍地走，安能辨我是雄雌？”

图书在版编目（CIP）数据

不朽的美：大风起兮云飞扬：许渊冲经典英译诗词：周朝－六朝．第一辑：汉英对照 / 许渊冲译．-- 北京：新世界出版社，2019.6（2021.6 重印）

ISBN 978-7-5104-6279-5

Ⅰ．①不… Ⅱ．①许… Ⅲ．①古典诗歌－诗集－中国－汉、英 Ⅳ．① I222

中国版本图书馆 CIP 数据核字 (2017) 第 100685 号

Songs of the Immortals

AN ANTHOLOGY OF CLASSICAL CHINESE POETRY (I)

不朽的美：大风起兮云飞扬

许渊冲经典英译诗词（周朝—六朝）

第一辑：汉英对照

译　　者：许渊冲
审　　定：王池英
责任编辑：李晨曦
特邀编辑：杨晓敏
装帧设计：贺玉婷
责任校对：宣　慧　陆诗婷
责任印制：王宝根　苏爱玲
出　　版：新世界出版社
网　　址：http://www.nwp.com.cn
社　　址：北京西城区百万庄大街 24 号（100037）
发 行 部：(010)6899 5968（电话）　(010)6899 0635（电话）
总 编 室：(010)6899 5424（电话）　(010)6832 6679（传真）
版 权 部：+8610 6899 6306（电话）　nwpcd@sina.com（电邮）
印　　刷：北京亚通印刷有限责任公司
经　　销：新华书店
开　　本：880mm×1230mm　1/32　尺寸：145mm×210mm
字　　数：55 千字　　　　　　　印张：4.875
版　　次：2019 年 6 月第 1 版　2021 年 6 月第 2 次印刷
书　　号：ISBN 978-7-5104-6279-5
定　　价：28.00 元